S0-AWM-829

A Note to Parents

Welcome to REAL KIDS READERS, a series of phonics-based books for children who are beginning to read. In the classroom, educators use phonics to teach children how to sound out unfamiliar words, providing a firm foundation for reading skills. At home, you can use REAL KIDS READERS to reinforce and build on that foundation, because the books follow the same basic phonic guidelines that children learn in school.

Of course the best way to help your child become a good reader is to make the experience fun—and REAL KIDS READERS do that, too. With their realistic story lines and lively characters, the books engage children's imaginations. With their clean design and sparkling photographs, they provide picture clues that help new readers decipher the text. The combination is sure to entertain young children and make them truly want to read.

REAL KIDS READERS have been developed at three distinct levels to make it easy for children to read at their own pace.

- LEVEL 1 is for children who are just beginning to read.
- LEVEL 2 is for children who can read with help.
- LEVEL 3 is for children who can read on their own.

A controlled vocabulary provides the framework at each level. Repetition, rhyme, and humor help increase word skills. Because children can understand the words and follow the stories, they quickly develop confidence. They go back to each book again and again, increasing their proficiency and sense of accomplishment, until they're ready to move on to the next level. The result is a rich and rewarding experience that will help them develop a lifelong love of reading.

WITHDRAWN

BLACK RIVER FALLS PUBLIC LIBRARY
22 FILLMORE STREET
BLACK RIVER FALLS, WI 54615

For Dinah,
with thanks
—M. L.

Produced by DWAI / Seventeenth Street Productions, Inc.

Copyright © 1998 by The Millbrook Press, Inc. All rights reserved. Published by The Millbrook Press, Inc. Printed in the United States of America.

Real Kids Readers and the Real Kids Readers logo are trademarks of The Millbrook Press, Inc.

Library of Congress Cataloging-in-Publication Data

Leonard, Marcia.
    Get the ball, Slim / by Marcia Leonard ; photography by Dorothy Handelman.
        p.   cm. — (Real kids readers. Level 1)
    Summary: Twin brothers play ball with their dog Slim.
    ISBN 0-7613-2000-8 (lib. bdg.). — ISBN 0-7613-2025-3 (pbk.)
    [1. Brothers—Fiction. 2. Twins—Fiction. 3. Dogs—Fiction. 4. Stories in rhyme.]
I. Handelman, Dorothy, ill. II. Title. III. Series.
PZ8.3.L54925Gg   1998
[E]—dc21   97-31376
                                                                              CIP
                                                                              AC

pbk: 10 9 8 7 6 5 4 3 2
lib: 10 9 8 7 6 5 4 3 2 1

Get the Ball, Slim

Marcia Leonard

Photographs by Dorothy Handelman

![M]

The Millbrook Press

Brookfield, Connecticut

I am Tim.

5

My twin is Jim.

We play ball
with our dog Slim.

I get my mitt,
the ball and bat.
I get the dog. . . .

Jim gets his hat.

I toss the ball.

Jim hits it far.

Oh, no! Oh, no!
It hits a car.

It hits a can.
It hits the wall.

I do not see
the ball at all.

23

But Slim will get it.
There he goes.

He finds the lost ball
with his nose.

He brings the ball
to me and Jim.

We pet and hug him.
Good dog, Slim!

31

Reading with Your Child

1. Try to read with your child at least twenty minutes each day, as part of your regular routine.
2. Keep your child's books in one convenient, cozy reading spot.
3. Read and familiarize yourself with the Phonic Guidelines below.
4. Ask your child to read *Get the Ball, Slim* out loud. If he or she has difficulty with a word:
   - Help him or her decode the word phonetically. (Say, "Try to sound it out.")
   - Encourage him or her to use picture clues. (Say, "What does the picture show?")
   - Ask him or her to use context clues. (Say, "What would make sense?")
5. If your child still doesn't "get" the word, tell him or her what it is. Don't wait for frustration to build.
6. Praise your beginning reader. With your enthusiasm and encouragement, your child will go from one success to the next.

Phonic Guidelines

Use the following guidelines to help your child read the words in *Get the Ball, Slim*.

Short Vowels
When two consonants surround a vowel, the sound of the vowel is usually short. This means you pronounce *a* as in apple, *e* as in egg, *i* as in igloo, *o* as in octopus, and *u* as in umbrella. Short-vowel words in this story include: *bat, big, but, dog, get, him, his, hits, hug, Jim, lot, pet, Tim.*

Short-Vowel Words with Beginning Consonant Blends
When two different consonants begin a word, they usually blend to make a combined sound. Words in this story with beginning consonant blends include: *Slim, twin.*

Short-Vowel Words with Ending Consonant Blends
When two different consonants end a word, they usually blend to make a combined sound. Words in this story with ending consonant blends include: *lost.*

R-Controlled Vowels
When a vowel is followed by the letter *r*, its sound is changed by the *r*. Words in this story with *r*-controlled vowels include: *car, far.*

Double Consonants
When two identical consonants appear side by side, one of them is silent. Double-consonant words in this story include: *mitt, toss, will,* and words in the *all* family: *all, ball, wall.*

Sight Words
Sight words are those words that a reader must learn to recognize immediately—by sight—instead of by sounding them out. They occur with high frequency in easy texts. Sight words not included in the above categories are: *a, am, and, at, brings, finds, goes, good, he, I, is, it, me, my, no, oh, our, play, the, there, we, with, you, your.*

BLACK RIVER FALLS PUBLIC LIBRARY
222 FILLMORE STREET
BLACK RIVER FALLS, WI 54615

DATE DUE

E Leo
Leonard, Marcia
Get the ball, Slim
11/98

WITHDRAWN